To my daughter Myla,
who has helped me realize
how beautiful this world is.

So the three of them decided
to play pretend.

"We would walk, jump, play,
and even dig holes
in the soft, fluffy clouds."

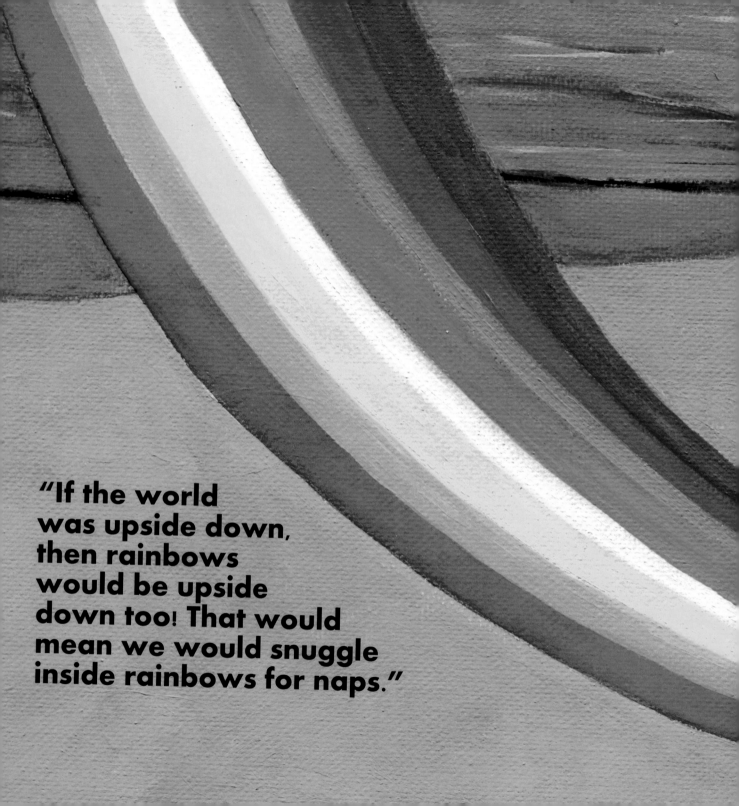

"If the world was upside down, then rainbows would be upside down too! That would mean we would snuggle inside rainbows for naps."

After we picked apples and oranges, we would play with the animals in the trees: chipmunks, raccoons, and squirrels."

"If the world was upside down, we would watch birds and butterflies fly by our heads."

"We would have the best view of fireworks! How many can you count? One, two, three, four and more!"

"It would be fun to drink water from a fountain. We would stand on our tippy-toes and go slurp, slurp, slurp."

"For good luck, we would drop pennies
in the fountain by throwing
them UP in the air."

"But when it did snow, we would catch snowflakes with our mouths facing down."

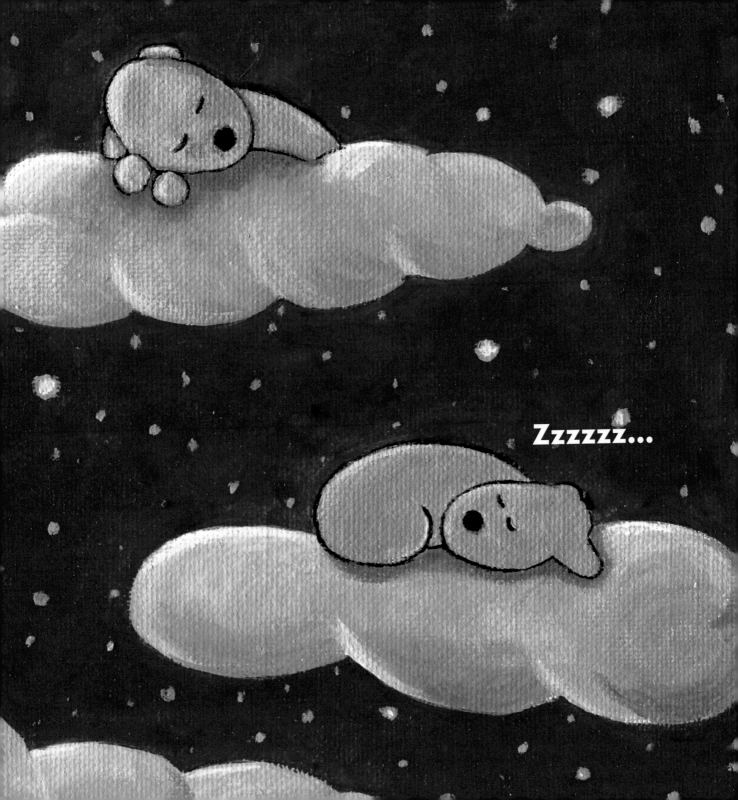